Valley Noir
Valley Blanc

JM BAYLISS

jmbayliss.com

Valley Noir Valley Blanc

March 2022 This book is a work of fiction. Unless otherwise stated names, characters and incidents are the product of the author's imagination and any resemblance to actual people living or dead or any historical event is entirely by coincidence.

ISBN 978-1-7397245-1-1

Mark's debut novel 'The Lucidity Programme', is a paranormal mystery. A best-seller, reaching #33 in its Amazon category. Chapter 1 is included at the back of this book. Available in paperback and e-book.

His short story 'Taste the Darkness', won the Henshaw International short story competition in December 2019 and can be found within this anthology of short stories.

His second novel, 'Rare Earth', is a dark thriller, set in the Welsh UNESCO World Heritage site valley town of Blaenavon. Chapters 1,2 & 3 are included at the back of this book. Available now in paperback and e-book.

In memory of my mother Mary
who loved telling me stories

Choose Your Moment and Your Story

2 minutes ☕ 5 minutes ☕ ☕ 10+ minutes ☕ ☕ ☕

Contents

Winner of 1st Prize in the Henshaw Press December 2020 International short story competition.

Taste the Darkness

I can't be sure what came first. The deafening thundering sound, the earth-shaking under my knees or the shockwave of hostile air and coaldust charging down the narrow tunnel towards our confined space. We were accustomed to coaldust, but nothing as frightening as that, filling our eyes, going down our throats and into our lungs. Then, in an instant, there was silence. It lasted a moment, before my little sister Gwendolyn started crying and calling my name. She had just turned seven and worked underground with me for only a few months. The fear in her young voice was palpable.

'Alwyn, Alwyn, where are you? I can't see! My eyes! What's happening? Alwyn, Alwyn!' I remember the sound of her little chest, desperate for oxygen, coughing and wheezing for all she was worth.

I managed to gasp a response, 'Gwen, it's OK, I'm here, feel my leg, I'm here up ahead of you.'

We found ourselves on our knees and elbows, partly submerged in sludge, inside our cramped three-foot-high tunnel. Gwendolyn's little fingers grasped around my ankle and she started to cry with relief. As she sobbed, I sensed her hand trembling as she gripped my leg as tightly as she could.

The strange thing was, my first thought wasn't a concern for her fear, but a hope that her tears would clear her eyes and her nose. I was eleven, and scared too, terrified, but I didn't want to frighten her any more than necessary. Having worked in the pit for five years they nicknamed me the *veteran drammer*. Drammers like me pushed and pulled the small low trolleys along the coal seam track, once the older colliers finished filling them with coal. Like many of the youngest girls and boys, Gwendolyn's job was *doorkeeper*, the men called them *trappers*. They opened and closed the haphazardly air sealed doors along the numerous tunnels.

Gwendolyn looked up to me, so I needed to stay calm - she depended on me.

A long time passed before the dust finally settled, our ears stopped ringing, our mouths cleared, and our dreadful dark tomb came into a grim focus. Gwendolyn had her small oil lamp, but I had nothing because I had been heading towards lights twenty yards in front of me when it happened. I'd heard the sound pitfalls make a few times over the years, but nothing like that - a completely different noise. Nor had I ever experienced the ground shake like that before or encountered such a dramatic surge of debris and dust. Right away, I realised, it must have been an explosion - a big one.

There was another reason why Gwendolyn couldn't see well earlier. She had a nasty gash on her right eyebrow. It was pouring with blood and her eye was swollen shut. My shirt sleeve was filthy, but I tore it off and made a makeshift bandage for her head. The bleeding seemed to stop.

We shuffled closer and huddled together, I realised we were trapped. The trolley I'd been pushing appeared almost entirely entombed. In the dim light, its steel rear wheels, barely visible, splayed out sideways. Hundreds of tons of coal and rock had crushed it. I'd been lucky, two seconds later, two yards further along and that would have been me.

A couple of yards behind Gwendolyn the roof had caved in on our side of the door she was attending. We were stuck in a soaking wet space, five yards long, less than one yard high and hardly wide enough for a grown man to crawl along.

Gwendolyn's voice quivered as she sobbed, 'Are we going to die, Alwyn? I don't want to die; I want my mam.'

Pulling her in closer to me I reassured her, 'We'll be OK Gwen. The rescue men from the pithead will have us out soon. We just need to sit tight, and they'll be here. We'll be fine, honest.'

Gwendolyn responded to my reassurance, yet her dusty cheeks remained streaked, and deep inside I desperately tried to reassure myself we would survive.

It was probably a good thing neither of us owned a watch. I couldn't remember if Gwendolyn had learned to tell the time anyway, she certainly couldn't read. Gwendolyn's light was an indication it had been a while since the explosion because it had slowly dimmed and eventually gone out. Nothing to see anymore, although we contended with the acrid smell of burnt kerosene oil and hewn coal which surrounded us. The explosion happened with such speed even the rats had no time to avoid it. We had company; I counted two of them crawling over my left foot before I managed to kick them away.

My teeth started to chatter, and my shirt clung to my back from the incessant drip after drip raining down on us through the wood-propped slatted ceiling. I couldn't see them, but I knew my hands would have been blue. Somehow, exhausted from fear and poor air quality we fell asleep, I'll never know for how long.

Gwendolyn fell fast asleep, although she twitched and whimpered in the crook of my arm. Soon afterwards, I awoke to a thudding noise, sensing it getting louder and louder. The noise came from near to where Gwendolyn's door once was - our way out. It felt like an eternity, but the thudding was relentless and rhythmical, they were digging us out. I woke Gwendolyn and for the umpteenth time as we sat listening, we said the Lord's Prayer out loud with our hands clasped together against our chests.

Then, in the darkness, voices, they sounded faint, but I was convinced I could hear voices.

'They're coming Gwen! I told you we would be OK, didn't I? Won't be long now.'

A terrifying blackness, no words could describe, had immersed us for hours and hours. We hadn't been able to see a hand in front of our faces since Gwendolyn's lamp went out, ages ago, and now, a tiny glimmer of light appeared. The relief was overwhelming and we both started screaming out loud. Whoever the men were, they responded, the tempo of their hacking and mandrills increased dramatically. The reassuring chink of light suddenly exposed more of itself and our eyes squinted with delight, before crying with relief and joy.

Gwendolyn's vice-like grip released from around me and she vanished, as I realised, they were hauling her, feet first through the emerging hole. Then my turn came, they pulled me through by my forearms and placed me on a coal trolley alongside her. I held her hand as they gave us some water and took us at a lightning pace to the lift cage, hundreds of yards away.

As we reached the ladders and rope lift, the men helped us off the trolley. I tried, but my legs wouldn't hold my weight to stand, cramp, cold and the fear in me must have deadened them. As they closed the door on the basket-cage to take us to the surface, I turned to one of the rescuers, 'What about my dad and my uncle Wil? They were up ahead of me hewing at the coal face.'

'We'll get them out soon Alwyn, they'll be OK.'

I never saw my father or my uncle Wil again.

Potent Karma

"So, how? Can someone? Anybody? Please tell me *how* she, *Sara what's her face*, does it? Impossible. She's not that good, not that brave, and definitely not that lucky. We call that cheating back in LA!"

"Thanks, *loser,* and it's Warricker if you don't mind. Not *what's her face* – Doctor Sara Warricker, to you."

My comments went down well, with chuckles all around. Yes, I had developed some astounding skills as a poker player, and grown some *stones* judging by the reactions. All in four months up to that point.

When the hand finished, the irritated Californian guy, sat with a face like a smacked arse two seats along from me, muttering to himself, on our ten-seater poker table at the Rio All-Suite Hotel in Vegas. The unimpressed dealer and referee both intervened, reminding *loudmouth* about table etiquette. He mumbled a begrudging apology, which I graciously accepted. Of course, I don't blame him, he had run into a poker freak – me.

That was my first visit to Vegas, my first-ever visit to a casino and my first-ever face to face game of poker, and all my opponents were men. It makes me smile just thinking about it. A surreal experience considering, I mean not just any old poker game, it was the World Series of Poker, the *main event* and playing for $8M.

All my previous poker experience came from playing *Texas-Hold-'Em* online, for ten cents a game. Breaking even every day after a few games was about as rare as rocking horse shit. 'Soft-Touch-Sara', my friends affectionately nicknamed me. The only *bluff* I ever successfully navigated took place somewhere in Snowdonia, and even then I needed a map. But one day, everything changed. My whole life changed.

I had recently returned from a mountaineering expedition in the Himalayas. I am not a mountaineer by any stretch of the imagination. I'm a doctor - and a bit of a free spirit. A pharmaceutical corporation funded a group of us to take a sabbatical and study the effects of hypoxia on the human body. Scientists, medics, and a few local fixers - there to keep us out of harm's way. What better place to research the deadly condition than in the foothills of Everest, where climbers die from hypoxia, amongst other things, every week. Sounds blasé, but I saved the lives of a dozen people during the three weeks I spent there in the prime, April, climbing season.

Four days before returning to normality and some much needed R&R in Kathmandu, a *Sherpa* mountain guide unzipped my tent door. He woke me up in a panic at 3.00 a.m.

"Miss Sara, Miss Sara, come quickly. You must come at once," he ranted.

I rummaged for my head-torch, threw on my only pair of trousers, a jumper, puffa jacket, a pair of unlaced boots, and stepped out into the bitter cold. *The Sherpa* led me across a rocky escarpment towards a scruffy looking multi-coloured Yurt. An old man stood waiting for me outside it. He bowed, placing his hands together against his chest as he did, whispered something, then opened the yak hide door for me to enter. I ducked my head and went in, to encounter an intense aroma of incense and oils, battling with the smell of a wood-burning stove, almost overpowering me. Handmade candles and small, incongruous LED lights surrounded the periphery. My eyes watered, and my throat started picking within seconds, as they adjusted to the acrid thin air.

There on a low straw bed, laying inside a half-open luminous lime green *Berghaus* sleeping bag, was a young woman that I recognised. Someone I recalled meeting when we first arrived at the tiny village.

"Bhavisana," he said, pointing a grubby finger at her. *"Bhavisana"* – in a quieter, concerned tone.

I could see her, and the reason for the commotion. Bhavisana was the twelve-year-old daughter of the man who opened the yurt door for me, the camp elder, his only child. He looked a grizzled, ageing man, with a face like a pair of broken-in oxblood

Dr Martins, and every other tooth either missing or black. Someone told me later, for forty years, he had personally saved the lives of hundreds of foolhardy mountaineers seeking an Everest summit for their sad CV's. Now, his daughter was extremely sick, with a fever, blotched skin, and a racing heart rate.

I examined her, immediately recognising the symptoms of sepsis - she was gravely ill, with an infected cut on her leg. The sepsis symptoms must have come on rapidly. Complications happen fast, and in her case compounded by the altitude. I needed to act swiftly if I had any chance of saving her. I pumped in a powerful antibiotic injection, combined with an IV drip, and we monitored her over the next 24 hours. Her life was in the balance for a while. Local women and children sat outside the yurt, with the freezing wind howling, I've no idea how they stuck the sub-zero temperatures. I could make out their incessant, gentle chanting, humming and occasional wailing. They all came to offer support and prayers – it was incredible, humbling.

Without a doubt, *someone* answered their prayers. Bhavisana's condition improved significantly by the next day, and she spent the remainder of her recovery in a medical unit at another camp as soon she could travel.

As I got my kit together to leave camp to go home a few days later, I received an invitation to a small ceremony, which took place inside Bhavisana's father's yurt, led by a local *Jhakri* - a Nepalese Shaman.

He looked like the father's identical twin, but with fewer teeth. They say the Solukhumbu District people revere and respect *The Jhakri*. I didn't understand a word during the half-hour ceremony, though I sensed a genuine spiritual experience – I got goosebumps and tingled. After the climax of the ritual, the *Jhakri,* with his magnificent headdress of peacock feathers, took me to the nearby river. He conducted one final cleansing spectacle in private, a *puja*, some Hindu act of worship, to honour their guest, *me*, and celebrate the healing of Bhavisana.

When the time came to leave the mountains, I felt invigorated – and *different* – hard to explain, but *different*. Bhavisana's father told me, "the *Jhakri* has granted you a wish. The wish will not last forever, but you must trust his word. Trust in yourself and you will find enlightenment and contentment." I thought to myself, *do me a favour*, but I remained respectful and professional.

The first few weeks back home were, well, beguiling, is the best description. I first noticed things changing when I began playing a few games of poker. I gave the games maximum concentration and had an urge to say a few silent prayers and to meditate. Religion was never a big deal for me, but things took on a new dimension. I won game after game with ease – ridiculous, I know. Sometimes I sensed a voice behind me, guiding my decisions. *"Believe. Trust. Accomplish. Be thankful."* The whole experience was hard to take in.

That went on for weeks, consuming me, playing for higher stakes, I never lost. Then I made an impulsive decision and entered the biggest poker tournament on the planet. Something compelled me to take things to new levels of concentration, determination, and self-belief. To challenge myself.

And Vegas was where I found myself, playing seven gruelling days of poker, meditating and reciting mantras to help me discover the level required to win the big decisions. On the final day, at the final table, there were ten of us left competing against each other for the $8M first prize. Before the final session started, Fox News interviewed me on TV, "Sara, is it true you have a Nepalese mystic in your corner? Helping you to make the big calls?"

"Rubbish. Do you news guys really believe in all that hocus pokus bunkum?"

As the game progressed and players fell by the way-side, I received my cards, with $3M on the line for fourth place, and went *All-In* with a pair of tens. A decent hand, but a huge risk for such a massive amount of money. *"Believe, believe!"* I implied I had a poor hand, a bluff, but it wasn't, and I 'got the hand through', knocking the other guy out.

In the end, lack of game time and mental exhaustion eventually got the better of me, my luck and belief ran out. I finished third winning a small fortune.

It felt like a dream, I looked around the small intimate arena, certain I spotted a familiar face in the shadows behind the cheering crowd on the *rail,* assuming it was just my imagination.

As I left the poker table the crowd applauded, giving me a huge ovation. With my poker chips in hand, walking away from the table to cash out, I noticed it – a tiny peacock feather softly fluttering to the thick pile carpeted floor.

The Unshod

Now I understand why. Why everyone I spoke to about this place all gave me the same expressionless look. Local people, often with plenty to say, who remained tight-lipped. Experienced people, older, wiser, with an understanding of something no one would dare talk about. Why didn't I listen to their silence and take the hint? Because I watch bullshit Discovery Channel conspiracy TV shows for hours on end, every day. Where everything remains a mystery and nobody ever gets hurt, do they? *That* is the reason. What a joke.

The comfort and safety of my sofa and the tactile feel of the remote control all seem like a million miles away. Now that I'm lost, stuck, alone. Too late - it's over.

I had decided to experience a beer or two in Wales' oldest pub, *The Skirrid* - the hanging pub - followed by a pleasant chat with the landlord, who offered to show me around the infamous former coaching house.

He led me back-of-house, near the stairwell, to the area where the hangings took place hundreds of years ago. A confined space with a thick darkened beam above, where dozens of men and one woman, all tried and convicted criminals, lost their lives. The woman claimed she was the landlord's mistress, so his wife concocted an irrefutable accusation of the theft of an heirloom to keep her quiet - permanently.

I found myself drawn, not to the solid oak beam, but the cold stone walls surrounding the innocuous-looking area. No trap door existed in those days. No sophisticated, weighted, and calculated 'long-drop'. Just a shove off a three-legged stool by the hangman sufficed. The poor souls, hands bound behind them, would lunge and kick furiously, searching without success for purchase on those surrounding stone walls, a toe hold, anything. Desperate to cling on to life for one more second. Until nothing. Until death comes, and silence, other than for the diminishing faint squeak of thick sisal chaffing on the burnished edge of a beam high above.

After the tour, as we wandered back to the bar, the stranger appeared. Over in the corner, reading his book, minding his own business. Apart from one brief moment, when he glanced over his spectacles in my direction as I approached. He smiled and muttered six words in his indistinguishable accent, "He's right, I have seen it."

That was the moment. Like a huge *Skirrid* spiders web, with him in wait, sitting at the centre of it, reading his book, and I tapped on one strand, sending him my vibration. My invitation. He guessed I'd go for it, he sensed it.

The distracted landlord had left me to scuttle off and serve another customer. "What did you see?" I asked the stranger.

"I beg your pardon, but I couldn't help overhearing something the landlord mentioned to you on your impromptu tour. About the shoes and the boots," the stranger replied.

"But the landlord doesn't know any more about *them* or where *they* are, he told me so," I replied. "He thinks it could be an old wives tale."

"That was what he said. But he knows more. He just doesn't want to talk about things or get involved. I don't blame him. He's only been here less than a year and he's got a business to run. He would have listened to the rumours by now."

The stranger knew why I came to the pub. He figured out that I had heard the rumours, and my morbid curiosity, combined with my pathetic dark hobby, got the better of me and I needed to find out more. But no one was saying anything – until now.

"You didn't finish telling me what you said you saw. Or where it is. So what can you tell me?"

The stranger put a bookmark into his book, closed it, carefully laid it down on a dry area of his table and said, "Dead men's shoes and boots. The ones that fell off in their frantic dying moments, lost in a desperate bid, flailing, and kicking to find a foothold with their last breath. They say the landlady at the time would collect them, take them away and *dispose* of them. She had a thing about their footwear, people say an obsession. And a myth grew up around her and her obsession. Like bad luck, a prophecy if you ever looked at her hoard. Well, only if you believe that kind of stuff. I don't, so I decided to find out for myself. I know where she hid them. I found the place. I have seen them."

I bought him a drink, accepted another in return, and we continued our conversation. I became more relaxed and even more intrigued. So when he offered to take me to the hiding place, I agreed in a heartbeat.

Still light, in the balmy June evening, the short walk from the Skirrid pub took us past my VW camper van, along a lane and behind two old cottages in the shadow of the Black Mountains. Part of me asked myself, why the hell am I following a complete stranger into a remote rural location with no phone signal, to find dead men's shoes. I never was risk-averse, and less so after a few beers. But *he, that,* was the reason I came to the pub. To satisfy my couch potato curiosity, to find answers, and a thrill. I couldn't resist.

He explained he rented one of the cottages that came with a decrepit barn and outbuilding, saying he had started to explore them three weeks earlier. We stepped inside the dingy building, assisted by one crappy flickering light bulb and our phone torches. Sheep and badgers had taken a shine to it long before us by the looks and smell of it. In front of me was the accumulation of decades worth of old farm implements. Saddlery, rakes, hitches, ploughs, hooks, all piled high and hanging on the walls. Out of place, an old rug hung from the ceiling to the floor, loosely nailed to a wooden joist that ran along the wall at the far end of the room. He pulled the rug down in a cloud of dust and threw it aside.

The dusty environment and the nervy circumstances caused my voice to lower to a whisper, as I coughed, hesitated, and asked, "I thought you said you had been here and seen this stuff before?"

"I did, but I put things back as I found them - I hate spiders," he replied.

Removing the rug revealed a cobweb strewn padlocked door, and one of the keys provided by his estate agent unlocked it. Shoving the door open, I ducked, to avoid bumping my head and even more cobwebs. We moved through the old doorway into a smaller room, six by fifteen feet with the late evening light trying its best to break through the filthy cracked window. Hay covered flagstone flooring supported a flimsy wooden ladder which led to a small mezzanine upper floor level. Looking down at my feet, I realised I had kicked the large pull ring of a three feet square basement door hatch, bolted down at each side.

At this point, I'm standing there thinking to myself, "*You're kidding me, right? No Chance.*"

"Don't worry, I cleared the dust and crap last time, I'll go first. You won't need to follow me down if you don't fancy it? Maybe you can see what you need from up here?" He said with confidence.

But I *did* follow behind him. Down some wooden steps, into a head high, gloomy void. The musty stench almost made me wretch. "What is that stink?" I asked.

"No fresh air for a long, long time. Combined with these I suppose."

He pointed to a three-legged stool. Neatly lined up all around and in front were half a dozen pairs of black leather shoes, boots, and one smaller pair of fine brown shoes with pointy toes, slender heels, and a fancy bow. Someone had placed the dainty shoes in prime position on top of the stool.

I moved closer and examined the various pairs of shoes. Finally, holding the small pair of woman's shoes, I turned to ask, "My God, surely these belonged to the woman they hanged? The landlord's, wrongly accused girlfriend."

But there came no reply. Silence, other than for the heartbeat pounding in my head. I looked again over my shoulder, I was alone, in the ancient basement of a forgotten barn, in the middle of nowhere, with a useless phone, and the wooden floor hatch silently locked shut above me.

Now as *I* sit here in the Skirrid pub, waiting in the corner, minding *my* own business, reading my book, gripping my bookmark in readiness, I glance up over my spectacles towards the opportunity that presents itself, coming towards me, and I mutter aloud six words, "He's right, I have seen it."

I Started but I Never Finished

I have been languishing here for decades, through every season, befriending passers-by and dogs whenever possible. Often wondering what to do with myself and what might have been if things had turned out differently for me. So many unanswered questions remain.

It all started to go wrong in early 1972 when they passed me over for that full leather version. You know, the black one with the chrome arms, opulent, comfy, ergonomic, high back and a swanky polished swivel base. Personally, I couldn't understand what all the fuss was about, but each to their own.

To this day I still blame that Magnus *'bloody'* Magnusson. OK, I realise it must be close to 50 years ago, but I can remember it like it happened yesterday when he first came to see me.

He noticed me immediately and said with great conviction that *Scandinavian simplicity* would prevail; the minimalist, timeless look as he described it. He even sat on me for half an hour whilst taking some *Fika*. He dragged me around for a bit and shook me from side to side; I think he was checking my legs. He was a bit rough with me if I'm being honest about it. Then he lifted me up, put me back down, stood back and looked at me adoringly with that cheeky Icelandic sideways glance of his. I should have known then he had a cold side to him. There was a clue in there somewhere, but I never got it. He just built me up, raised my expectations and then let me down. How could he have done such a thing to me?

He even said the table would definitely get the gig. '*The contestants will need somewhere to put a jug and pour themselves a glass of water,*' spoken in his rather posh Scottish accent. He was full of crap; I mean they only had two minutes; they were hardly likely to be wasting twenty or thirty seconds swigging Evian's finest, were they?

He told me, that he and the producers had everything worked out: the format, the catchphrase, the lighting, the music, but I was going to be the star of the show … well, me and a countdown timer clock with an electronic buzzer. Oh, that's right, I remember now, he said '*We'll also need four more similar chairs, although maybe with a slightly lower back, for the contestants who are waiting for their turn you see.*' Yes, I was going to be *the one*, me, out front and in the spotlight!

Look at me now, I'm a shadow of my former self. My frame had to be welded twice and I've been repainted three times, then they spray me with

WD40 every winter. It's quite sad really, I've got standards you know.

I'd been hanging around optimistically for all those years, I couldn't let go. Most of my friends, including the parasol, gave up on me ages ago and moved on. You can't buy loyalty can you, but at least the table has stuck by me, that's been a blessing. Maybe if they'd given me some cushions or at least a comfy little seat-pad, back in the day, I might have stood more of a fighting chance, but we'll never find out, will we?

A glimmer of hope emerged in the early noughties when the current presenter, John Humphries, came on the scene. Rumours of a revived retro look were abounding, but no, the Welsh aren't renowned *early adopters* let alone retro lovers, are they? Now an Englishman called Clive is in charge, when will all end?

Foolishly, I wondered to myself, what if I had some castors fitted, or *had some work done?* No, I learned my lesson. I've been led up the garden path far too many times, and I suppose it won't be the last time either.

It - Rubbish, Recycling, Upcycling

Twelve years had passed by, not one painless day amongst the thousands of days. In all that time *it* had never seen the light of day - nothing but darkness. *It* just sat there, wrapped in a dirty cloth, surrounded by balls of rolled up, tea-stained, Western Mail newspaper pages - broadsheets in those days - placed in a PG tips tin and hidden under the floorboards. Where *it* had been left, but not forgotten about, following *its* return from Belgium and VE day celebrations.

Forgotten, that is until yesterday. Because yesterday, everything changed. Yesterday was a gut-wrenching day. Yesterday all the emotions came flooding back from twelve years ago. Yesterday, right there, in all its digital glory for everyone to see – just like it was yesterday.

After everything was resolved back then, *it* was almost thrown away into a reservoir, and nearly discarded like rubbish, in the bottom of one of the new plastic wheelie bins we started getting from the council at that time. *It* failed to find the water or the bin. Nostalgia, foolishness, sentimentality, insurance, call it what you will, either way, *it* ended up back in the tin, unable to 'read *its* way out'.

For a time, three years ago, *it* almost got *it*self removed, for everyone's sake, 'probably for the best'. Almost, wedged in between the walls of an old double radiator, mixed in with a few other metal items and almost dropped at the household re-cycling tip for melting down, that was the plan. But *it* remained in the tin, still under the floorboards still struggling with the crossword.

Then came the news, yesterday, no one mentioned it, simply some vague information appeared way down on the BBC Wales news mobile phone feed, concerning what would soon be happening.

Today finally arrived, feelings of twelve years in the planning, but in fact, there had only been twelve hours to think.

That face could never be forgotten, even after all this time. Staring across at those features in the dock for six weeks, looking at those cold eyes incessantly, trying to learn something, hoping to find an explanation, see a weakness, or genuine remorse. But finding nothing but pain and anguish.

Today outside HMP Prescoed; the tin – gone; the Western Mail paper – gone; *it* saw the light of day earlier; *it* had been cleaned and readied and loaded. A fumbling, twitching hand, on *it*, ready to use *it*. Early release and resettlement is the official description. Human recycling of sorts.

It never left the coat pocket. The pathetic image, of the decrepit, aged target, averted the long awaited decision. Instead, *it* was taken into work, permanently decommissioned, some small steel rods and plates welded around *it*, a maple handle fashioned and fitted over *its* barrel. The head came from a discarded old dumbbell. *It* has been completely transformed, upcycled. Now *it* sits in a toolbox in the garage at home, *it* might be used one day to hammer in a nail or two.

687 Red Days

Today is '1' - day one - a fresh start, full of high hopes and expectations - I hope. Thank God day 687 is behind me, and the previous 686 for that matter. Everyone else in the team drew the same conclusion yesterday whilst we enjoyed a muted celebration, welcoming the arrival of the new Martian year.

Last year took its toll on us in more ways than one. We were eight; now we are four. The back end of the year devastated us. Lack of concentration, carelessness, complacency, and a deadly rockfall. That's why the mining corporation brought us 40 million km in seven months, and pay us the big bucks - to take risks for exploration rights to the huge mineral rewards. For some people in our team, the bonus incentives outweighed the calculated risks and they paid the price.

A NASA scholar needs to come up with some 'day/month names' instead of just 'numbered days', something other than yet another statistic to live our lives by until they extract us in, yeah, 200 days. What's that in Martian weeks? God only knows. I miss my family back home and I miss Wales; it pains me to think about them.

My mind wanders as I drive this $2.7 billion rover vehicle across the baron topography. How many Ferraris and Aston Martins combined is that? I guess I can afford one of each when I return home. I need Martha to nudge me and keep me focused before we both become another statistic. We have encountered crevices and subsidence in the past, enough to swallow us both and this 'one careful owner' piece of kit.

"Hey Martha, two minutes to the new exploration zone. From here it looks like all the others - red, dusty, and innocuous, other than for that little bump or crater the drone picked up on its fly through. Not great images though. Ten metres across I'd say, probably a pile of Martian shit, or maybe a sandcastle that the Venusians forgot to kick over when they left after a summer holiday a million years ago."

As we rumbled along, Martha replied from the next seat, "You're full of it today aren't you – crap that is – Martian crap! Keep your eyes on the road partner."

Her confident New England accent often keeps me on-point, but my mind regularly wanders. We have our regulation tasks, daily processes, and geological procedures, but the bottom line is, being on this God-forsaken planet is nothing more than like being stuck on a gigantic oil tanker or container ship. At least those guys get to play table tennis, go fishing, lay in the sun on a break or stop at a picturesque port. People make mistakes here, it's easy to understand why; like that big one last year. My shift changed; it could so easily have been me.

Martha jolted me back into life, "Coming up ahead. I'm getting my navigational ping, we're almost on the location. Remind me why did this spot flag up to the guys back home before we sent our drone?" she asked.

"New data from Launch Base Command Centre, and because they did the calculations, the geo-mapping, the perfect storm they said. They reckon this has all the hallmarks of the 'good stuff'. This is prime mineral real estate potential right here. But the satellite imagery would never clear itself, electrical interference - or something, pixelations, lucky for us our little drone went in low. Even that decided not to play the game as well as it usually does."

Martha replied, "Great. And the location is also less than half a kilometre from last years' accident. Someone back home at LBCC is loving this area. Stay focused."

Why the electrical interference and imagery pixelation I asked myself? Why did the drone work marginally better? A tease. I had a sense of excitement. For us, it was a rare occurrence for a slightly off-piste, unsubstantiated foray, to break the house rules and the monotony. All we had to rely on was dodgy drone footage, nothing much else from L.B.C.C.

Large rocks ahead brought us to a cautious halt. As we stopped, we made some visual checks, stepped out and clipped on our handheld spectrometers. No fake minerals got past those things.

Martha raised her arm in the direction to our right. "I think that little mound, 50 metres away, is the bump the drone captured. From here it looks like the rim of a small crater to me. Race you!"

As we approached the elliptical-shaped mound, our normally dependable instrumentation started playing up. I reminded Martha, "Plenty of oxygen - three hours' worth, so nothing to worry about with the readings, but we must keep a close eye on the time, OK?"

"Sure. Understood. Three hours."

Martha wasn't kidding. She had pushed on whilst I checked my oxygen level. Twenty metres ahead of me, she had made the short climb up the gentle slope of the mound. As she did, she turned 180 degrees back towards me and yelled, "It is a crater, Jesus, you won't believe this! Oh my God!" With her voice shaking, and the audio breaking up a little, Martha had never sounded so excited since we arrived. Not since launch two years ago.

I joined her, and we stood side by side on the rim, in silence, gazing at what presented itself a few steps ahead of us.

"Is this for real, or is something wrong with our oxygen/nitrogen mixture? Or maybe the low-pressure status in our suits has changed?" I checked the oxygen and the time once again, "Martha? Hello, speak to me?"

When I looked around; Martha was gone. She had ignored me, shuffled down into the base of the crater, and walked towards the remarkable spectacle before us. As I paused for a moment, observing the scene, we shared a surreal moment. Impossible, but it stood there right in front of us.

I made my way down to Martha at the base of the crater. We both looked up in wonderment at the ten-foot-high structure. Hewn vertical boulders, carefully positioned, capped by a massive, disc-shaped rock. For some reason, the solar winds and dust storms had chosen to ignore this tiny location. The Martian regolith soil should have submerged the obstructive boulders, but to our surprise, they appeared unimpaired, like someone had constructed them yesterday. The entire scene remained protected by some strange anomaly. I could hear my heart pounding inside my helmet, and sensed my adrenalin eating up the air supply.

"I know what this is. Or at least, I've seen something identical to it back home in Pembrokeshire. *Pentre Ifan.*"

"What the hell is Pentre Ifan? A thing, a person or a place?"

"All three I suppose. A neolithic burial chamber, five or ten thousand years old. But more importantly, what the hell is it doing here? How did it get here? Who put it here... and who the hell is buried under our boots?"

A Hint of Recognition

Søren Lemvig adored social media. He found Facebook and LinkedIn an irresistible tool to reunite distant friends and rekindle old relationships, although he struggled with Twitter and Instagram.

A dramatic event impacted his affectionate opinions when an earth-shattering *LinkedIn* message etched itself into his pale-blue irises. The 'optical lightning bolt' despatcher was someone whom Lemvig vaguely recollected meeting thirty-one years ago, in northern Spain. A brief, casual acquaintance, yet someone with devastating first-hand knowledge about something dreadful he once did. Something he hoped and prayed, for decades, would never come to light again.

~

Gregarious, semi-retired Lemvig's enthusiastic chat continued, as he helped retrieve forty bright yellow balls before he waved off his personal coach.

Lemvig spent his summers in an ultra-modern, eco architect's dream, near Fuglevik, south of Oslo, a deft 'drop shot' from the surf. Kicking off his 'red clay dust covered' Nikes, he picked up a towel, a cold drink and scanned his iPhone - one missed call, six WhatsApp's, and one email notification via Linkedin. The new abstract email message heading read: *Remember the San Sebastian car crash, 1990?*

Lemvig coughed and spluttered his iced tea. His white Fred Perry would need a good wash. In an instant, his churning stomach and pounding heart suddenly collided somewhere in the middle. Emotions surged through him - panic, fear, anxiety, and reading the email still awaited him. His mind ignited like a bad psychedelic dream.

"Gud i himmelen!"

~

Six weeks earlier, Dominic Milne and his wife Sian enjoyed a long holiday in San Sebastian and set off on a *Camino pilgrimage* hike to Santiago de Compostela. Milne last visited the area thirty-one years ago - the northern Spanish coast reminded him of their native Wales coastline.

In September 1990, Milne and two of his keen amateur cycling clubmates used San Sebastian as a base to tackle some tough classic mountain climbs in the Pyrenees. Their finale and relaxation involved spectating a stage of a famous professional cycling event, *La Vuelta a España*.

Today, Milne and Sian found a busy café in one of the central squares. They needed a hearty breakfast to set them up for the carb-burning day of walking confronting them. Milne stepped inside the dingy establishment to find the toilets, and on his way out he spotted some old memorabilia, in and around banquette style dining booths and a bar area. Adorning the walls were a proud and dusty display of bullfighting *banderillas*, football scarves, club pennants, and a multitude of tired-looking foreign currency notes pinned around the bar.

Close by, a gurgling Gaggia machine spat steam, before expelling a perfect regulation trickle of aromatic coffee. Behind the cutlery, he spotted some magazine cuttings and an array of faded but treasured polaroid pictures. He almost missed them; someone wanted to keep the pictures safe by tucking them behind a piece of protective glass, stained by tobacco and decades of exposure to the enriched wafts of Columbia's finest.

One of the pictures caught his eye, stopping him in his tracks. He took a closer look, and to his astonishment, he saw himself in the picture taken back in 1990, posing outside the café. With him were the then café owner and a TV pundit - a once-famous Spanish pro cycling champion.

Milne struggled to hook the faded photo out from behind the glass to examine the photo. Originally taken decades earlier, the picture's initial reluctance to move suggested its status as a 'semi-permanent fixture'.

At last, holding the memento between his fingers, he realised he was looking at not just one, but two polaroids, the second one appeared slightly stuck to the back of the first. He smiled as old memories of waving other freshly taken polaroids in the air to dry them, and hints of a *chemical developing aroma* came flooding back to him.

The hidden rear picture looked almost identical to the front one. But also captured in the hidden photo were Milne's two cycling club mates Matt and Stuart, a Norwegian lad wearing a green T-shirt and the same former pro cycling champion/TV guy. Everyone, holding beers aloft, cheering and celebrating the end of the race stage. They had befriended the Norwegian whilst cycling for a few hours before the pro race concluded. He looked at the rear of the second picture and to his surprise, he found everyone's names written there, including the Norwegian's name - Søren Lemvig.

"Bloody hell!"

A *Camino* is a long arduous trek; people choose various routes to make the iconic hike, and for different reasons; religious and spiritual. All routes converge on the historic city, and all happen to share one other thing in common - they provide time to think. Milne found himself doing plenty of just that for the next two weeks.

~

No internet existed in 1990. Mobile phones were in their infancy, reserved for business executives and no text messaging yet either – or any budget airline flights existed back to the UK after the friend's cycling trip. Instead, they endured a vomit-inducing, twenty-four-hour, Bay of Biscay ferry journey, with no cabin. Topped and tailed with a van full of bikes and smelly cycling kit.

Matt contacted Milne a week after their trip, "Dom, I've just read cycling weekly. Sad news, the TV pundit outside the café, he's dead! Killed in a car crash. Hours after we met him. Incredible."

The media reported his Maserati convertible lost control on a mountain bend, after colliding with a motorcycle. The car left the road and rolled three times. The TV guy died, along with the motorcyclist, a gory mess. Confusing rumours started circulating, suggesting the TV guy was not behind the wheel when the sports car crashed. Police wanted to interview a tall blonde man, wearing a green T-shirt, seen in a village nearby swapping into the driver seat and roaring off, minutes before the accident.

The police retrieved *the driver's* fingerprints, blood samples and strands of green fabric, together with measurements of skid marks from the wrong side of the road. But *the driver* vanished. The entire incident remained a mystery. The official recording of the accident stated *culpable homicide,* and the case remained open.

Milne and his friends recalled listening to the Norwegian, chatting to the TV guy outside the bar about cars, boasting of his rallycross expertise back home in Norway. They recollected him changing imaginary gears and pulling handbrake turns with their beer bottles. Neither of them remembered his name, although all agreed, judging from news reports, he was behind the wheel of the crashed car. They thought no more of the incident and wrongly assumed surely the police tracked him down in the end.

~

Milne revelled in the hot challenging hike. As they walked together he chatted with Sian about their plans for the future. Ideas for a business start-up idea could not get off the ground and always stalled, because sourcing funds proved a tough struggle - with something else impacting matters. Milne gambled online, managing to accumulate a large gambling debt. They kept separate bank accounts, and for now, Sian remained oblivious. He felt trapped in a deep, dark hole, with no sign of a ladder.

During their walk, Milne's burning curiosity led to him researching the tragic motor accident from thirty-one years ago. He trawled dozens of online records, translating many with an app on his phone, and discovered that investigators never found the driver of the sports car. The Spanish police failed to identify the mystery blonde driver, and over the years they arrested no one.

Milne Googled *Søren Lemvig, Norway,* and dozens of hits instantly popped up, *"Yes, there he is. No doubt about it"*

Cropped, receding grey hair, and he now wore fine framed round-rimmed glasses – although still a striking resemblance after thirty-one years. The image on his phone didn't lie, a certainty for the guy they met. The same guy in the polaroid wearing the green T-shirt and without a doubt, the same guy who crashed the car - technically still on the run.

More digging showed images of Lemvig socialising with Norwegian celebrities and minor royalty, clearly a wealthy man. He owned a lucrative stake in his family's thriving North Sea oil industry business. Milne read another article concerning the *trillion dollars Norwegian sovereign wealth fund* and how the fund was entirely based on oil reserves.

Milne, mused, *"Bloody hell. No wonder he's minted and mixing with Norwegian Royals. I wonder if they know he's on the run?"*

By the time Milne reached Santiago, a plan bubbled inside his head. He would make contact with the old acquaintance not seen or heard of for thirty-one years.

~

Lemvig's fingers fumbled, infuriating him as he accessed his Linkedin account, desperate to open the private messaging section, where he found the more detailed message. Someone called Dominic Milne claimed they met thirty-one years ago, after a cycling event in San Sebastian.

The message read, *"Hi Søren, long time no see, thirty-one years? Guess what I found on a recent trip to a bar in*

San Sebastian? This attached old polaroid photo was taken of us after watching the pro cycling race. Heart-breaking about the Spanish TV guy in the picture with us though eh? I have the original, with the names written on the back. Are you interested in buying this from me? Plus another thirty-one years of silence from me? Here's my mobile number."

The message tantalised further, "Let's speak soon shall we? Mid-mornings are best. Maybe we can come to a mutually beneficial arrangement? Best wishes for your future, Dominic."

After a restless night of soul searching, attempting to conjure up excuses, denials, and contemplating the wider stark implications, such as imprisonment in a Spanish jail, Lemvig got his head together. He made the call.

Milne stirred his coffee, deep in thought, alone at his gym. Brimming with determination he had already reconciled himself to go through with his nerve-racking plan – and then his phone rang. He answered it, exchanging superficial pleasantries with Lemvig.

"OK Søren enough of the crap, you have two minutes. I'm going to make you a one-off future-proofing offer. You need to take it and we can go our separate ways again."

Lemvig paused, "Blackmail is a high stakes business, the UK police take it extremely seriously."

A clamminess surfaced on Milne's hands, and his mouth needed a sip of water. Some parking tickets and a drink driving ban ten years ago were the worst misdemeanours of his entire life. He expected resistance from Lemvig, but knew the Spanish police would pounce on his startling revelations. Lemvig's validatory call motivated Milne, toughening his persistence. His reckless personality trait caused his gambling problems, and now he had crossed the line. Excitement and adrenalin also played a part, and nothing would stop him.

"Oh yeah? Well, culpable homicide is a *deadly* high stakes business, and the Spanish police take a serious view of that too. So, Søren, let's make this easy for both of us. I'm not asking much from a man of your resources; all I want is eighty thousand pounds in cash, for let's call it 'a valuable piece of art' shall we? Take it or leave it, I'll save your mobile number and call you tomorrow, goodbye!"

Overnight, Lemvig recognised the catastrophic exposure facing him. Humiliation and a 'steel bunk bed' terrified him in equal amounts. He saw no alternative and he would agree to pay the money. A paltry eighty thousand was peanuts to him, a tiny fraction of what he would earn in a typical year.

When Milne called the next day, Lemvig's simple, sullen response was, "OK, how do we sort this out?"

They agreed a trusted family lawyer, an old friend of Lemvig's, would visit the UK to meet Milne. He would conclude the arrangement with no knowledge of its dirty history and carry out the simple instructions.

Two weeks later Milne met the lawyer at a Cardiff hotel. Eighty thousand pounds in *twenties* fitted with surprising ease into a large envelope, tucked inside the small black messenger bag handed to him. In return, he exchanged a sealed envelope containing the polaroid. The lawyer had instructions to pass 'the document' to Lemvig, unopened, on his return.

~

Milne, still an avid cyclist, peddled hard, well into one of his regular, solo road bike rides, passing around the quiet, spectacular, and exposed Hay Bluff in the Welsh Black Mountains. He continued climbing the hills narrow road, planning a sharp descent towards town. Quads on fire, his heart rate monitor kept pinging 'in the red' warnings, as his lungs worked overtime, sucking in every available millilitre of oxygen. Coupled with the headwind, an anonymous white van, keeping its distance from him for the last two miles, went unnoticed.

Hay Bluff road has several 'sketchy' points with severe 100ft drop-offs to one side. Milne's heart-monitor spiked for a second at 220bpm, then fell silent.

Rescuers discovered his body at the base of one of the drop-offs, an hour or so after the white van hit him. Investigators later calculated the impact from behind at over 60mph. Detectives searched in vain for months and never found the van or its driver.

Five days after the *accident*, two of Dominic Milnes old cycling friends, Matt and Stuart, arranged to visit to pay their respects, offer support and reminisce with Sian.

An hour before they arrived Sian started to look through some of her husband's belongings, unable to face touching anything until that day. She never snooped or even used his iPad, but knew his password and logged in to search for some old pictures that she expected to find - to show his friends. Once again, she broke down in tears. This time the emotion resulted from accounts on the iPad displaying the shocking evidence of his secret gambling habit. To make matters worse, hidden in his wardrobe, behind his cycling gear she discovered an envelope with almost eighty thousand pounds inside. The envelope also included a compliment slip from a Norwegian law firm, handwritten on the slip read simply, *"Mr Milne, £80,000."*

When the two friends arrived, she decided to show them the money and the compliment slip, "Matt, did you know Dom gambled? Or why he kept eighty grand stashed in an envelope in his wardrobe? Did you? Please be honest with me."

Matt's jaw dropped and he stumbled getting his words out, "Never heard of that before Sian, and never realised Dom gambled until this minute. I'm stunned."

The astonished look on Stuart's face told her everything, "Me neither, Sian, honestly, that's an absolute shocker to me. I would never have guessed. What's that all about?"

Sian decided to park the discussion after debating her disturbing finds and made some mugs of tea. She talked a little more about the funeral and the inquest,

"What a mess, everything is so complicated. Things will take months to sort out with the police and the coroner."

The cycling friends sympathised and wished they could do more to help.

As the atmosphere lightened up a little, they went through some old cycling photo prints, and some others in folders on the iPad, Sian *mirrored* them onto her smart TV screen. As they reminisced, they all laughed and joked at many of the photos - but a shocking surprise hit them when they came to three images in particular. The first two images showed the front and rear of an old polaroid pic, the third image showed a screengrab pic of a LinkedIn profile - Søren Lemvig's profile.

Matt almost squealed as he spoke, "You're kidding me. Stuart, that's him, isn't it? That's the guy. The guy in the car. It's him, *Søren Lemvig*."

Reunited

Made whole, rejuvenated, is this place for real
Ethereal topography, sensory, surreal
Cold and darkness extinguished, sunshine and
warmth prevailing
Hard to articulate, inner calm and peace entailing

Happiness and contentment, both partying
with my soul
The time's arrived, relief at last, nothing
more to control
Optimism and hope, since discovering my destiny
My confidence undaunted, evident for all to see

I wondered if they'd take me when I knocked on
heaven's door
An open arms acceptance, and a green
light to explore
Anticipation, trepidation, questions soon resolved
I'm feeling tranquil, intrigued, and
undoubtedly absolved

Sadly, it's been chaotic, there's an endless
human stream
Of course, no one's ever ready, to go and
'join the team'
We know it's not discerning, and not all
of us immune
Waiting, praying, most are hoping, it's 'maybe
no time soon'

Hints of recognition, old friendly faces they appear
A familiar form emerges, elegantly drawing near
Young, happy, beautiful, unmistakably no other
Decades have passed, yes it's her, hands reaching
out, my mother

Peace *Time*

After a heavy Saturday night, and ignoring three early morning missed calls from unknown numbers, William Duberley, governor of Cardiff prison wandered into his corner shop. He picked up a paper and scanned the headline *Unapproved life-changing drug trial at HMP Cardiff.* The article, from an alleged reliable source, incredulously claimed the prison's population of just under eight hundred hardcore inmates, had become permanently reformed overnight.

"What, the…?"

Duberley read on. It went on to say, *"During the previous week an outrageous sabotage of the recent innovation of a full-scale prisoner flu-vaccine programme for all inmates took place."*

Reports described a substitution of the flu vaccine with an alleged single application synthetic drug, which induced a permanent effect on the brain's prefrontal cortex, causing complete eradication of any triggers for aggressive or malicious thoughts and behaviour. Amazingly, the recipient would simply become normal, friendly, and considerate with no other side effects to their personality or physicality. The vaccination switch claimed to have turned the inmates into saints.

Compared with mood-altering, daily dose tranquillising drugs, offering short-term effects and obvious physical side effects, the journalist suggested the vaccine substitute offered a completely different proposition.

Just as Duberley started to read more of the jaw-dropping front-page article, his phone began ringing again in his pocket. As he fumbled for it, he caught sight of three more newspaper headlines: The Sunday Express was *The Silver Bullet*, The Sunday Mirror went for *Peace Time*, and The Mail on Sunday header read *The Evil* Shot.

On Saturday night, just before their deadlines for their Sunday papers, all editors had received a letter with a memory card enclosed. The memory card contained pictures and video footage outside and inside Cardiff prison of a masked nurse swapping the flu vaccine vials for the alternative drug and delivering them overnight to the prison surgery's large refrigeration unit. There was also a file on the SD card containing detailed corroborative information of the drug's capabilities and a description of what took place in the preceding weeks.

It explained during WWII the Nazis developed an early version of the synthetic drug, now known as

93ACE. The drug had been an experimental antidote to an aggression inducing 'fighting drug' created and administered to thousands of German troops. In South America in the late 1940s, a scientist further refined 93ACE, with more work recently conducted in the UK. The wonder drug had then been successfully, surreptitiously, retested on dozens of unsuspecting UK subjects over the past twelve months.

The SD information went on to state that the prisoners in HMP Cardiff had all been 'beneficiaries' of the new wonder drug and by now would have started to experience behavioural changes immediately after receiving the drug. The people behind these claims made no financial or political demands. They said like many people in society they were sick and tired of seeing the country being eroded by the criminal class. A solution now existed for society's problems. Convicted violent criminals, tagged and remand prisoners would all be reformed in an instant; a permanent removal of the risk they posed, saving billions of pounds and thousands of lives.

The information ended with the statement, '*Wait and see the truth, ask the governor at HMP Cardiff for facts and statistics over the coming weeks. You will hear from our organisation through the media again soon.*'

Duberley took a deep breath and finally answered his phone to one of his prison Supervising Officers, James Pugh. They briefly discussed the worrying news articles, then agreed on immediate plans for riot avoidance, a temporary lockdown, and a news blackout. Duberley didn't have all the facts and his head was spinning, so they agreed to discuss things in an hour once more information became available.

Just before they ended the conversation Pugh commented, "Wil, do you realise that over the past four days we've not received one report of a single fight or a disagreements on any of the wings? It's unheard of. Seriously, it's like a church in there and I honestly can't see us needing a lockdown. Something is going on."

Something was going on; Twitter was going nuts; human rights groups were outraged claiming UK government complicity due to a forthcoming General Election. Even Brexit remainers pitched in, suggesting HMRC immigration control involvement. A Russian hacking group 'chancing their arm', tried to get in on the act by demanding a Bitcoin ransom before unleashing further similar events using other drugs with far more alarming or sinister effects.

Instead of going back home for breakfast, Duberley picked up a bunch of newspapers and drove straight to his office inside the prison. Reporters jostled for positions and camped themselves outside the prison gates on Knox Road. Duberley wondered what next, where next, who would explain what was going on, was anything genuinely going on inside the prison or would it be the biggest fake news scenario of the decade so far.

On route he played half a dozen voice mails, thankfully very few people had his work mobile number. Notables asking for urgent call-backs included the CEO of HM Prison and Probation Service, expected to come under intense pressure for answers from further up the food chain. The prison doctor went on standby and headed for the medical wing. The urgent to-do list of priorities grew.

Nobody thought of this as a false alarm. Duberley needed immediate answers and would need to prepare an initial statement to keep the wolves at bay. Adrenaline kicked in, and his hangover rapidly disappeared.

~

At his small farm and yoga retreat in the Welsh Black Mountains, James Seymour, the wealthy, hedge fund director and retired former Chairman of Life Tech Pharma, sat in the kitchen of his beautiful barn conversion. As he observed the news story unfold, he smiled knowing he was the man behind the controversy.

Seymour carried a huge chip on his shoulder. Despite his many millions and with too much time on his hands, he made several failed, blunt attempts to barge and buy his way into politics. His attitude irritated far too many well-placed influential door openers. As a result, for him, the door to becoming an MP and climbing the political ladder to power remained firmly closed to any mainstream party hopeful of winning a seat in parliament.

This man harboured aspirations to mould and change society to how he wanted it to be as soon as possible. Seymour would never consider going down the time-consuming official route of lengthy clinical trials, drug testing and years of waiting for approvals from the MHRA and FDA, only to face rejection due to human rights activists and risk-averse politicians. He was unfamiliar with failure, his arrogant vision for the future would probably include a bronze statue of himself erected in a park somewhere.

At 11.00 a.m. Sky News received a flat 'no comment at this stage' from the prison governor as he walked through the gates. Sky said that a further statement was due at midday. Meanwhile, the news team lined up two experts at the news HQ, one an American Professor of pharmacology from Cambridge University, the other a retired Nobel prize-winning German genetic engineer.

The pharmacologist, hired to debunk the story, keenly explained, "The ludicrous wild claims being proffered from the memory card could not be achieved. Yes, an abundance of technical details about NMDA receptors and DNA catalysing enzyme effects on the brain could be found on the internet. But so what?" Then, hedging her bets, she said, "So far, no hard evidence exists, and I don't expect any meaningful evidence confirming the dramatic claims." But her body language and tone of her voice appeared more hopeful than expectant. A large seed of doubt was growing in her head.

The German geneticist appeared less circumspect, stating, "Similar stories have circulated for decades about the work of the Nazis in this field and in the past some evidence has emerged. But this new speculation is at another level, it is feasible, and no rules and regulations existed back then. Who knows what they created which has not yet seen the light of day? Remember jet engines and nuclear fission, where do you think those ideas originated?"

James Seymour listened to the so-called experts intently. A brilliant scientist in his own right and an even better marketeer, he also spoke several languages fluently, enabling him to build his pharmaceutical business and sell it to an American conglomerate for a huge fortune several years ago. These days he preferred to relax with Gussie, his third wife. To keep busy and for fun, they shared a thriving wedding venue and yoga retreat business. In reality, the business was a front and the distraction he needed to pursue his other less salubrious scientific work. In between times, they travelled the world visiting exotic countries, occasionally visiting Gussie's grandfather just outside Montevideo in Uruguay, the only remaining member of her near relatives. Three years ago they went back to Uruguay for the funeral of Gussie's grandfather, who thought the world of his granddaughter. He was reclusive, with a Danish passport, but with a distinctive German accent on the occasional Skype calls that Seymour joined.

Gussie came from a small family and was an only child. Her parents had passed away, but grandad lived to a ripe old age. After the funeral, some possessions passed to Gussie, including a small apartment near the Santa Lucia River, a garaged, dusty but roadworthy 1951 Mercedes-Benz 220, some trunks and a small library of books and documents. Helping to clear things out, it soon became obvious to Seymour from the books that linguistically, grandad's German was better than his Danish and it was here Seymour stumbled across details of a perilous journey in early 1945 from Germany to South America. He also found some remarkable handwritten scientific journals, notebooks, and documents. He made copious notes and took photographs of the pages in the books that interested him.

~

Midday at Cardiff prison gates, Governor Duberley stepped out with his pre-prepared statement. It read, "Following recent media speculation I can confirm that all our residents are in good health. Our prison doctor has not treated any unusual or unexpected illnesses today. Our flu vaccination programme went ahead last week as planned. We are confident that all staff followed procedure and systems and processes within HMP Cardiff were robust and continue to remain in good order. This is an excellent establishment with a good track record and a team of dedicated staff. We will update you on any further developments. I will not be taking questions. - thank you."

Inside the prison, other than for doors opening and closing you could almost hear a pin drop; subdued voices - no ranting, no gesticulating, no tribal banter, a far cry from the usual alpha male hostile challenging environment. Just friendly, calm, peaceful faces everywhere.

The original flu-vaccine manufacturer instructed the prison doctor to conduct checks and tests on the residuals of the batch of vials. He confirmed to Duberley the batch of 'vaccines' given to the inmates was not flu-vaccine. The vials contained an undetermined substance. Prison officials and government ministers expressed deep concern. All came to the same alarming conclusion, they needed to find who did it, how and why they made the switch and the efficacy and dangers of the drug. Some politicians were heard muttering, "Let's hope it's for real."

~

Seymour remained in his kitchen, finalising some cryptocurrency payments for services rendered. In the past on his travels, whilst paying fixers to gain agreements for medical trading licences in third world countries, he learned how to make plenty of friends in low places.

Gussie appeared in the doorway, smiling. She picked up the TV remote and turned it off, and said, "We need to talk, now!" She got straight to the point, explaining that she knew exactly what had happened, and asked her husband, "Have you forgotten my German is almost as good as my Spanish?"

She knew what Seymour found from the day they cleared out the apartment in Uruguay, but thought nothing of it. She didn't want to get into a slanging match about it and drag her grandfather's false Danish name through the mud. Now, her narcissistic, megalomaniac husband had well and truly lost the plot. She had always been loyal to him but knew she enjoyed the lifestyle far more than she adored him, and enough was enough.

Having watched from afar, the secret planning, dodgy meetings, and phone calls, she sensed things coming to a head. But didn't know if Seymour's original plans included transparency with the drug findings and to tell the world about the drug and possible positive applications, or if he was going over to the dark side. She now had her answers.

So, after plenty of thinking time, Gussie decided to cut and run, giving Seymour an ultimatum. Her lawyers received a sealed letter from her containing damning information that would put him away for years, to be opened in the event of her 'sudden death' or disappearance. She wanted a divorce, a large settlement, to keep the farm and for him to agree to an immediate move to be nearer his children who lived in London. Destroy all the evidence associated with 93ACE, hand over to her half of every penny that he owned, and she would never see him again. Oh, and there would be no media update today or any other day. In the eyes of the world, it would all be fake news from Russian hackers and a mystery virus believed by the prison pastor to have been the work of God.

~

Several weeks later, James Seymour visited London and sipped a coffee in silence whilst waiting to go and meet some of his hedge fund business associates. A middle-aged woman came in and sat on a stool next to Seymour. In her American accent, she said good morning and they both exchanged a few pleasantries.

After a few moments, she smiled startling Seymour by lowering her voice, and using his name, "Mr Seymour, the organisation I work for has taken a great interest in your work in Cardiff. Your creativity is impressive, to say the least, and we would be extremely interested in having a discussion with you. It appears that we have similar goals and aspirations."

Five minutes later, having postponed his original meeting, Seymour and the woman got into a car waiting outside.

She instructed her driver, "Take us back to Nine Elms."

The location of the new US embassy in London.

Stranded

Being surrounded by the vacuum of outer space for as far as a radio telescope can see accentuates the audible feedback. A perfect, smooth, synthesised voice issues *her* amiable instruction: *'21-11-2023, Celeste, begin your digital voice-activated recording at the bleep...bleeeep.'*

After a moment's pause to compose herself, Celeste begins to speak in her soft mid–west American accent.

OK, well, where do I begin? So, to whom it may concern is as good a start as any I guess. Moments ago, I encountered a scraping noise on the hatch door. The sound is becoming a more distinct intermittent knocking noise. Before I go to investigate, I am concerned this may well be my last and only message.

For me being an astronaut is a complex, exhilarating, stressful and dangerous career choice at the best of times. Today, I've been circling the beautiful planet Earth at 7km/second at an altitude of 475km for 12 days. For the past 18 hours, I have witnessed the total unexpected annihilation of the entire human population. This dreadful aberration included my family, friends, colleagues, and fellow countrymen. A vision beyond comprehension, like a bad, bad dream. I'm left feeling bereft and numb. All I possess today are my training, the human spirit, a strong desire to survive and my trust in God. But for now, I'm here to quickly describe my perilous situation and try to find a solution. I'm done crying, I can't bear to think about what may have happened to my family anymore, it's crippling my ability to think straight.

I observed a shimmering purple, fluorescent glow encompass Earth, enveloping it for 16 hours. This has since vanished, along with all communication from the planet. Hundreds of messages and endless data streams were reaching me in the beginning, for a couple of hours. Desperate distress calls from around the globe, maydays from submarines, military bases and political HQs and a neighbouring manned space station - all diminished. Now, there is just silence. Everything has ceased and has surely been extinguished - somehow. I just don't know how or what happened - but I've seen the appalling images. People simply dropping like flies. No one is left alive, anywhere. I remain uncertain whether the cause is a natural phenomenon or from an outside agency. Probably the latter. Then twenty minutes ago I thought I heard a scratching noise, coming through one of the aft bulkheads. I'm leaving my seat and heading the 10 feet to the airlock hatch behind me and preparing for the worst. I guess a

Smith and Wesson isn't deemed a necessary accessory at Kennedy Space Centre.

If this is still recording, I've stepped into my spacesuit, entering the airlock now and sealing it closed behind me. I'm shaking. Can you hear that... knocking? Is that for real? I'm opening the seal to the outside. OK, the hatch door is open.

Oh my God – I'm looking at another person suited up out there! Wait! One moment. I'm looking at...myself? The other person is calling me, towards *her*, the other person *is* me. There's another me! I'm following *her*, on my harness.

'Celeste please refresh and resume your voice-recording after the bleep...bleeeep'

A Glimmer

Wil Richardson displayed a year-round wind and weather-beaten complexion - a tanned shade of rouge. He would argue the sweet, perfumed aroma of fresh alfalfa hay on a man smelled as good as any aftershave. That, combined with his dusty pick-up truck, often loaded with bales of silage and two Welsh collies, betrayed his primary occupation.

At just over six feet tall, and a former rugby player, the size of his hands meant dropping the ball was a rarity back in his playing days. Outdoor manual work proved a far better regime than most gyms for Wil.

Wil and his wife Emma paid off their mortgage three years ago, well ahead of time. Bi-folding patio doors to the rear of their cottage opened out to a spacious south-facing decking. It offered stunning views of the Welsh Black Mountains with a stream running past the end of their garden. Over the years, they had worked damned hard and their idyllic rural farm was now more fun than work.

A Sunday spring morning dawned and the re-cycling boxes outside their side door over-flowed with discarded empty cava bottles, countless lager cans and one empty bright blue spirit bottle. The last of their friends left in the early hours, so the remainder of the clearing up began. The dishwasher needed filling and the remnants of some party poppers needed sweeping up, along with a couple of bespoke anniversary banners which had fallen onto the kitchen floor tiles.

"Wil, where on Earth did they dig out the old pool pics of us for those banners?"

"Brilliant, I don't think I'd squeeze into those tight blue Speedo's these days though, would I?" Wil laughed as he said it.

"Oh, I don't know, you still scrub up, and I always liked you in those budgie smugglers." Emma winked at Wil, still her mischievous self. Even though the previous night ended up as a late one, she saw it through, life and soul of the party – as always.

Their sons, Haydn, and George, both in their early twenties had popped in for half an hour or so, said hello, then headed back out. The boys left claiming they didn't want to send the average age at the party crashing down.

Wil and Emma had made a successful transition from farming to glamping and outdoor pursuits. Increased bookings, thanks to Emma's shrewd marketing talent, meant a new shepherd's hut would appear almost every month at the base of the sweeping mountains.

Haydn and George mainly ran the farm, but Wil still kept an active role in helping them. Emma set up the simple but enticing website and bookings portal for the glamping business and could run the various social media accounts in her sleep. Forty-nine-year-old Emma enjoyed a long and successful background in marketing and PR, often taking on some profitable ad hoc marketing projects, alongside running the glamping business. A smart move – she had the best of both worlds.

Three days after the party, the couple experienced an unexpected and radical change to their lifestyle. Emma was heading home late one evening from their campsite business near Crickhowell. For weeks incessant rain looked like it would never stop. The high water table, and fresh rainfall took a while to drain in the vale where they lived, near to the River Usk.

It was typical mid-April Welsh weather – unpredictable and unpleasant. Torrential rain on the roof of Emma's van made listening to the radio almost pointless. The windscreen wipers made a racket on their maximum speed setting. On-coming headlights dazzled, creating reflective blurs off the wet road surface.

Then, the unthinkable happened. With no time to react, the steering-wheel whipped through Emma's fingers, breaking two of them. A huge roadside pool of standing water caught her little van and dragged it off the road.

A split second later her 'white box' was caught in an uncontrollable slide, nosediving down a muddy

30-degree bank. The loud noises of scrapes and bumps from boulders, bushes and saplings drowned out the screams inside the van. It careered downwards, towards the river, before ploughing head-on into a beech tree and flipping over on its side. The crumple zones and airbags worked perfectly, absorbing most of the obvious impacts, sending the chalky airbag dust all around the inside of the van.

A thick heavy beech bough occupied most of the passenger side and part of the driver side of the van. The pierced, laminated glass windscreen, squashed inside the van, wrapping the glass around the intruding piece of the tree, curiously framing the wood like a piece of trendy installation art.

Ed Sheeran stopped abruptly long before the end of his track. Emma lay in silence, other than for the hiss of the leaking radiator; the wipers also came to a stop - ripped off and crushed like matchsticks. The seatbelt, soaked red with blood, did its best to suspend her as she slumped sideways – motionless.

Two young lads were taking shelter from the downpour at a nearby bus stop, regretting not wearing decent coats. Their playful banter stopped and facial expressions changed and they gave out a collective, "Whoa," as they witnessed the shocking accident. They sprinted over the road, slid, and scrambled down to the van and could see Emma trapped inside the steaming overturned wreckage. As one lad called for the rescue services the other did his best to check on Emma. He tried in vain to tug her out, but the van lay flipped over onto its driver side, with her jammed inside and bleeding from a head wound. They needed help.

Two sets of blue flashing lights arrived almost simultaneously within ten minutes of the crash. The firemen cut Emma out and paramedics strapped her neck-braced slender frame to a stretcher. Taking great care, they dragged her back up the rain-soaked muddy bank, through the open doors of the waiting ambulance vehicle, before blue lighting her to the nearest hospital. The gurney wheeled Emma into A&E – alive but unconscious.

~

Wil had attended Emma's bedside at the hospital in Abergavenny twice a day, every day for the past three weeks. She remained in a coma and he tried his best to keep a lid on his anxiety, perpetuated by his inability to contribute anything to her progress. All he could do was be there.

He was on first-name terms with most of the medical staff, and they knew all about him and the woman he'd spent most of his life with. When Wil was elsewhere, he and Emma – *that nice farming couple* – would sometimes come up in sober conversation between some of the hospital staff members.

Livestock on farms can't take holidays or sick days. Animals need feeding, mucking out and caring for every day. But both Wil's sons, Haydn, and George were at his side whenever they could, all sharing the anguish. Most of the time they sat in silence, looking up every time a doctor walked past – just in case of some news.

The doctors told Wil they were cautiously optimistic that Emma would pull through from the coma, but it might take weeks – or maybe months. The MRI scan showed the initial medical treatment to reduce the swelling pressure on her brain, caused by a blood clot, had proved a success. Now it was a question of time.

Friends and family all agreed if anyone were capable of pulling through – it would be Emma. She was a petite, fit, and healthy woman, a regular jogger, in training for her first-ever half marathon. Combined with her gritty determination, everyone genuinely believed she would be fine – sooner rather than later. She was bubbly, chatty, Emma, *Mrs Organised* – of course she would be fine.

~

Going about his business every day as normal and keeping himself busy, proved the best way for Wil to help try and take his mind off things. But it was a struggle. He threw himself into the farm work - repairing fences, improving the potholed access roads damaged by the brunt of the recent rainfall. A bucket of asphalt in a pothole rather than a new front suspension strut - always a no brainer for most thrifty farmers. The rangy, energetic man thrived on being active and getting stuck in.

Barely a minute went by before he again thought of Emma or hoped for a phone call from the hospital with some positive news. The family WhatsApp group pinged with a constant stream of positive thoughts and updates to keep each other sane.

Wil was also deeply concerned for his two sons wellbeing – they doted on their mother. The constant worry exhausted him, his appetite had vanished and every night he fell into a deep sleep. Then a few weeks after Emma's accident, an unexpected disruption to his sleep pattern occurred for two consecutive nights.

For as long as he could remember, Wil experienced what he described as *pretty crazy dreams*, maybe once every couple of months. Typically, he would be half awake, half asleep, almost controlling the direction of the dream. The dream often caused murmuring aloud, sometimes followed by screaming. Both were a signal that inside Wil's head he was experiencing the threat of violence.

Emma would always try to nudge him awake, before the murmuring escalated into anything more disturbing, or could reach any dreadful conclusion that the dream may have led to. They would often joke about it the next day and think nothing of it. Wil looked into it once, mentioning it to his doctor, and discovered the medical description for his night-time episodes was lucid dreaming.

"You've eaten too much cheese again love," was often Emma's standard response.

Wil later Googled 'lucid dreams', and discovered they were a common occurrence for some people and could be disconcerting – for both dreamers and their partners.

Without Emma to rouse him from his sleep for the past two nights, Wil experienced more unusual lucid dreams. Again, he felt alert and engaged in the current dreams, but they were not his normal, scary, and violent dreams. Instead, they took on a new dimension, becoming much harder to comprehend and far more compelling.

~

Emma's mother Maud died several years earlier, and Emma's dad died when she was a little girl. Like most children with one parent, Emma had a close relationship with her mum, and it devastated her when she died after a short, unexpected illness. Wil was like a son to Maud, and he thought the world of her. She was a lovely person and they grew extremely fond of each other over the years. At half-term and summer holidays, Emma and Wil would often take the children to the whitewashed cosy family cottage in Pembrokeshire, stay with Maud and gather with the rest of Emma's family. They were good times.

Over the years, Emma told Wil countless stories about growing up in Pembrokeshire and her fun times with her older siblings and friends, roaming around the stunning coastal paths and coves. Emma said most days she came home with a salty sheen on her arms and legs from the fresh sea breeze.

~

Hospital visits with Emma often consisted of playing her favourite music, reading her favourite books and magazines aloud, narrating through sets of old photographs and talking about his work that day around the farm and the campsite.

One evening Wil was searching through a box of old photographs, to take to Emma's bedside, optimistically assuming she could hear him. He found one photo of Emma with her mother Maud. On the visit to see her, he recalled an occasion when Emma became upset. She told him about the time she lost her mother's beautiful solitaire diamond engagement ring, a cherished family heirloom. She explained that her mother owned a fish and chip shop in Fishguard, and would always leave her engagement ring on the bedroom dressing table to go to work, wearing nothing other than her wedding ring. As a little girl, Emma loved to dress up in her mother's clothes, shoes, and costume jewellery, kept in a jewellery box. She loved to gaze at herself in the mirror pretending she was a grown-up.

On that particular summer's day when Emma was about ten years old, her mother went to work, leaving her at home with her grandmother. Emma's siblings were much older and always out. She was upstairs playing in her mum's bedroom, dressing up again. There was a knock at the front door and her grandmother called upstairs to tell Emma her friends had come for her. They wanted to know if she would join them to play on the nearby beach, where they planned to look for crabs in the rockpools.

An excited Emma got changed out of her mother's clothes and ran downstairs. She rushed and quickly grabbed her things and a little fishing net. When they reached the beach, Emma's best friend commented on the ring Emma had on her finger. Only then did Emma realise that in her haste to join her friends she had forgotten to take off the engagement ring.

There were no more than a couple of small fluffy clouds in the sky; the girls were laughing and having a lovely time. After a couple of hours of having fun with a bucketload of crabs, the tide rolled in and time to go home.

As Emma put her sandals back on, to leave the beach, to her horror she realised she was no longer wearing her mother's ring. It must have slipped off without her noticing. With tears rolling down her face and a knotted, sick feeling in the pit of her stomach, she and her friends searched for ages, turning over every pebble and looking underneath every shred of seaweed. Without success.

The time came for the long trudge home, head down swishing at flowers on the side of the lane with her bamboo fishing net along the way. A heartbroken Emma imagined the look on her mother's face when she told her what she had done. Her mother didn't speak more than the occasional word to Emma for days, often seen dabbing tears from her eyes. Emma would look to her mother waiting, hoping, for her customary affectionate glances, but none were forthcoming. Her mind kept swirling back to the beach and wanting to turn the clock back.

As the weeks went by, her mother's attitude changed, the smile returned and she forgave Emma. Just one of those silly little childhood mistakes, but it stayed with Emma for many years afterwards. She never forgot the look on her mother's face. She knew the ring was so precious to her mum because her dad had died three years earlier and Maud never got over losing him.

~

At home, the stress of Emma's accident began to tell on Wil. Exhausted from pushing himself too hard with too many hours on the farm and shuttle trips to the hospital, the following night he fell into another deep sleep. He recently started having strange dreams, and the strangest thing of all was Maud began appearing in them. The dreams took on a new dimension since Emma's accident and for some inexplicable reason, Maud's influence got stronger and stronger.

After the two previous unsettled nights, Wil found himself in his half awake and half asleep lucid state of unrest. He was revisiting the same recurring dream. And he was not in the same full control of the situation compared to over the years with his regular lucid dreams.

On the previous two nights, he could not conclude the dream – he got stuck. Tonight, the sensations were significant and much stronger. He thought he could sense and smell a sea breeze on his face and hear the waves over the side of a cliff edge coastal path that he was being led along. This place reminded him of somewhere familiar, in Pembrokeshire. He felt so certain of its proximity to the sea, it was palpable. His legs strode along, his feet slipped on the soft narrow coastal path and his arms brushed the undergrowth as they swung at his sides. Everything appeared real to him, including a woman up ahead of him, leading him along the path. He tried hard but couldn't make any ground to catch up to her. As the dream progressed, he thought he could almost reach out and touch the woman – she appeared vaguely familiar to him. Yet every extra effort to get one step closer proved unsuccessful. He called out to her several times. and then she turned her head, looked back, and smiled at him. He recognised a young *Maud* and this time Maud was controlling the dream, not Wil.

He could hear himself asking her, *"Where are we going, Maud? Where are we going?"*

Maud turned, and in her unmistakable soft Welsh voice replied, *"This way Wil, come this way - we're nearly there."*

In the distance, he could see a tall red and white striped lighthouse. He knew this place, from visits with Emma and the boys. Together Wil and Maud scrambled around a narrow rocky bend that dipped a fraction towards the water. They were still high up on the cliff edge, and at this point, Maud stopped and pointed in a precise direction down below them, towards the base of the cliff where it met the sea. She pointed to an inaccessible, small inlet, with layer upon layer of narrow rock shelves recessed into the cliff face above the high tide mark. Some resident seals barked and bobbed in the water just in front of it.

Once again, Wil heard Maud's distinctive voice telling him, *"Now, over by there - can you see?"*

Wil knew exactly what he needed to do.

~

Maud was long gone. Wil's eyes opened. He stared up towards roughly where he thought the rafters could be on his bedroom ceiling. The blackout blinds made the room so dark he had no idea what he tried to see or what time it was. The solitary sound he could hear was his heart beating in his head, as his clammy body struggled to recalibrate after his experiences moments earlier. Reaching one arm over to check the time, the dazzling iPhone glare in his hand told him the time, four a.m. and reaffirmed no missed messages or calls.

Wide awake, he jumped out of bed, skipped his usual shower and shave, got dressed back into the same clothes he wore the night before, and headed out through the door.

Wil drove the usual twelve minutes to his campsite business office in less than ten. An urgency overwhelmed him as he rummaged through his pockets fumbling for his security keys and alarm fobs.

He opened his lock-up, disarmed the alarm system and loaded his pick-up truck with everything he needed.

Two-and-a-half hours later, with the sun trying its best to make an appearance, Wil parked in the public car park near the Strumble Head lighthouse, set on a spectacular island outcrop on the craggy Pembrokeshire coastline in West Wales. The clear sky exuded a violet-blue tone, with a liberal sprinkling of stars, and to his relief, the Welsh coastal wind seemed tolerable.

He hauled his kayak off the rack on the back of his truck, pulled on his wetsuit, helmet, surf boots and buoyancy vest. He put the paddle and kayak on its little wheelie trolley and pulled it along the cliff path for four hundred metres. Wil found one of the handful of places where he knew it was OK for him to descend in safety, almost a hundred feet to the water, and get into his kayak.

He paddled around the headland for almost half an hour into the strong offshore breeze. It seemed as though everything pushed against him - the wind, the tide and the current - even bits of brown seaweed impeded him. Every little wave the tip of the kayak skimmed and bounced over, and every paddle stroke, sent a cold wet spray into the air then backwards onto Wil, but it felt good, he didn't care.

He closed his eyes for a moment and imagined it was the same breeze he thought he experienced hours earlier in his bedroom. Two curious young seals popped their heads above the water nearby to check out their visitor. Wil smiled and paddled on until he came to an inlet that looked familiar. He pondered for a second or two, but he thought he had seen this inlet from high above when he visited here with Emma and the kids. As he got a little closer, he spotted the high tide mark and recognised this as the place he needed to get to.

The rising sun cast a long silhouette from behind the outcrop of cliffs to the water's edge. It made looking into the dark shadows tricky and judging the rocks and ledges even trickier. Luck came to his aid, the currents and the waves became more favourable for him, enabling him to pull himself up on a slippery green ledge and hop out of the kayak. He stood up shivering, with seawater and drippers running off the end of his nose, then caught his breath and looked around him. There was not silence, but an eerie peacefulness. A special moment – Wil, his kayak, and nature. For the first time in weeks, he felt invigorated.

The lighthouse sat way over his shoulder in the background and for now, until the sun rose higher, its lamp would continue rotating a powerful beam of light every thirty seconds or so. Upwards, the partially hedge-lined cliff edge coastal path protruded with a perilous drop to where he stood.

As his eyes readjusted, he looked just ahead, then shuffled sideways a half a metre more as a fine adjustment. He waited, looking ahead in anticipation of the beam of light coming around once again from behind him.

Wil stared hard at the dark rockface where he had looked moments earlier, and there was no mistake, absolutely no doubt, he had seen a glimmer of a reflection. Something glinting and shining back at him from within the rockface in front of him. He slid his cold wrinkled index finger into a tight crack in the rocks and scooped out the glinting item. A solitaire diamond ring.

~

Wil's visits to Emma continued as normal throughout the rest of the week, every day he would sit by her bedside talking and reading to her. Being as gentle as possible, he would also slide the ring he found on and off her finger. One afternoon as Wil held Emma's hand, whilst she wore the ring, he thought he sensed a slight reaction or a squeezed response from her.

"Emma? ...*Emma*, please do that again."

She responded to him - she gently squeezed his hand again.

He burst out of the door and ran the short distance to the near-by nurse's station. He frantically explained to one of the senior nurses what just happened. On taking a closer look at Emma's monitors and data history, the nurse noticed some slight changes in the electrical activity monitors.

It felt like an eternity, but when the clinicians finished their work, Wil moved closer to the bedside to look at Emma. Expecting to say his usual 'see you tomorrow' to her as she lay there passively, he saw an unexpected flickering and opening of her eyelids as she said his name, "Wil."

It started with his legs, then his arms and hands – everything trembled. His words seemed trapped – he couldn't believe what he witnessed. Maybe the turning point? She was awake and alert.

After an emotional hour and some polite cajoling from the staff, Wil left Emma to rest. When he got to the door of his cottage, all he remembered was leaving the hospital and putting the key in the door – nothing else about the journey home.

The next morning Wil returned to find Emma sitting a little more upright. Before the birth of the children, her dark hair was long and curly. But now shorter and straighter, and someone had brushed it for her. She had some colour in her cheeks and looked much better. Her bright blue eyes widened, and she smiled as she saw him coming.

Wil kissed her on the cheek, and in his softest voice asked, "How are you doing?"

"I'm fine, *ish*. I feel a bit weak and tired. But something weird happened, I think I had a strange dream. Mum was in it telling me that you have something important for me - and then I woke up."

An emotional Wil held her hand and said, "Yes I do, take a look."

The little object that once held such emotional value, lost for decades, again sat on Emma's finger. Despite having lost weight during the harsh effects of the coma it still fitted much better than as a little girl. She looked down, shaking her head from side to side, her eyes and mouth open wide as she recognised the beautiful ring she lost all those years ago.

The shocked expression on Emma's face changed to one of elation as she smiled again and started to laugh. She stared at the ring, and asked, "Where, how?"

"I'll tell you later, it's a bit of a story."

~

After a slow frustrating process, Emma's strength and mobility eventually made significant improvements. Three weeks later, they made a nostalgic drive to Strumble Head and wandered hand in hand along a short stretch of the coastal path. As they walked, Wil had a sense of *deja vu* and shuddered when Emma turned and looked back at him; she was the image of the young Maud, even her voice was similar.

After a ten-minute gentle walk, filling their lungs with fresh sea breezes, they reached the exposed cliff edge high above the inlet. The light was perfect, and both the sky and the sea looked bluer than ever. Wil did his best to explain the whole thing to Emma as soon as she left the hospital, whilst also answering a barrage of questions. She stood on the clifftop smiling, with a strange sense of calm and relief to feel healthy again and to have the ring back in the family. Emma chose to wear the ring that day and every couple of minutes she found herself touching her finger to check, ensuring it was still there.

Emma realised she had come full circle, as she gazed way out to sea and simply mouthed the words, "Thanks, Mum."

About the Author

Mark's parents dropped the 'Jonathan' in favour of Mark almost immediately and he once forgot how to spell his Christian name several years ago - easily done. He is originally from the former Welsh mining town of Blaenavon, now a famous UNESCO World Heritage Site attraction.

As an apprentice, he survived electrocution, whilst drilling a hole in the floor of a flooded milking parlour, before going on to qualify as an aeronautical design engineer. He then spent most of his career in key accounts, designing and selling office interiors to blue-chip clients. His near-death experience decades earlier was surpassed when his career nearly ended abruptly – permanently. He was almost shot in the head at point-blank range with a Magnum .44 by an over-exuberant client whilst at a hospitality event in Sweden!

His award-winning short stories and other works can be found in national magazines and websites or published in other short story collections.

To relax he's recently ridden Tour de France alpine cycling climbs, hiked the 'Camino' across Northern Spain to Santiago de Compostela, snowboarded Mont Blanc's Vallée Blanche and once managed to outrun a herd of rampaging cows across his local Welsh mountains. He is secretary of the Hay Writers Circle and a dedicated yogi.

He lives in Wales with similar views to the characters in his valley noir books.

Acknowledgements

All my editing and feedback friends. A bunch of amazing people who kindly gave their time to read my work and help me. Not forgetting all my friends at The Hay Writers Circle for their constant enthusiasm and support.

The anonymous judges who awarded me the first prize in the Henshaw competition! They boosted my confidence enormously.

With special thanks to my wife Anne – she has spent hundreds of hours listening to my ramblings, reading, and correcting my work.

RARE EARTH – JM BAYLISS

Minerals, Greed and Death.

Today, murderous fraudsters have replaced the Victorian slave-driving coal masters in a famous Welsh valley town. Jason Price and Declan Ryan, make an astounding discovery that will rock Blaenavon. Struggling to make ends meet, three hardworking, unsuspecting sheep farmers assume the disused coalfield grazing land they own on a mountainside is worthless.

A geology professor and his vicious land-grabbing associates possess incredible information, having secretly discovered that the farmland, which surrounds a UNESCO World Heritage site, is a geological freak. Scattered amongst the millions of tons of coal spoils are precious rare-earth mineral particles – worth more than gold. People are paying with their lives for their silence. That is until Lauren Eaves, a gritty, young Australian geology student turns up to disrupt the fraudsters' plans, risking her own life in the process.

Available as paperback or e-book.

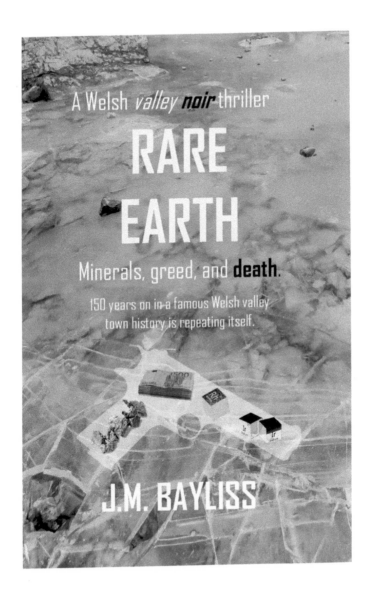

A Welsh *valley* *noir* thriller

RARE
EARTH

Minerals, greed, and **death**.

150 years on in a famous Welsh valley
town history is repeating itself.

J.M. BAYLISS

Rare Earth

Chapter 1

Cold Heart

Blaenavon, Wales - February 1973

I t's getting dark, I wanna go home now Jason. I've had enough, my hands hurt, please, *please*, I wanna stop and go home. I want my mam."

Rhys could barely feel the warmth of the tears as they streamed over his taut rosy cheeks and mingled with the snot dribbling from his runny nose.

Irritated by the annoying outburst Jason swooped, plucked the wet red bobble hat off his little brother's head, and flung it across the frozen pond. "Yeah, well I'm off, you can go home on your own. You'd better fetch that first though."

At the end of a harsh winter week, the high and exposed Keeper's Pond endured an incessant, biting north-easterly. The centuries-old irregular-shaped pond, about the size of three large football pitches, once served a long gone mining community as a reservoir. That week the expanse of deep water transformed into a shimmering pane, surrounded for miles around by the ethereal topography of *talc dusted* heather mounds, with not a single tree in sight. It looked like a moonscape – with sheep.

Late on a quiet Saturday afternoon, the two young Price step-brothers played at the pond, two miles over the mountain moors from their home in the Welsh coal-mining town of Blaenavon. The boys wore wellies, bread bags over socks for extra warmth, knitted woollen gloves - frozen rigid, and parkas with rabbit-pelt brims and rubber-lined pockets.

The eldest, eleven-year-old Jason tormented and bullied eight-year-old Rhys relentlessly, the same as he did most days. As a toddler, Rhys suffered brief spells in a hospital due to his asthma. A misguided Jason always felt devoid of a fair share of affection and attention growing up, often taking things out on his little brother. The vindictive, disturbing cycle perpetuated, as Jason's volatile step-father and vicious leather belt responded to Jason's behaviour with great regularity. No amount of whining from his wet, and cold brother would resonate with him that day at the *Keepers*.

Rhys wailed even louder, trudged off the snow-laden bank, and gingerly shuffled his way across the ice towards the awaiting bobble hat, to a spot where they played earlier. They had practised jumps and attempted 360-degree mid-air spins, neither landing them with any success, ending up with wet backsides and even colder hands. As he shuffled, he rubbed behind his left ear where the bendy wire arm of his steamed up NHS glasses kept digging in. The ear rubbing discomfort always became more noticeable when something or someone, usually Jason, upset him.

When Rhys bent down to pick up the hat, Jason yelled from behind him, "Hey Rhys!"

Rhys turned and spotted a large chunk of rock, the weight of a bag of sugar, looping through the air. It must have taken every ounce of Jason's strength to hurl the heavy rock as high and far as it went, landing with a hefty thud at Rhys's feet. The boys had thrown dozens of smaller, similar-shaped rocks earlier, which all landed, and chattered along the ice with the hint of an echo. Not on that occasion. The sharp-edged rock became embedded in the ice as cold mountain water oozed upwards all around it. Straight after the initial thud came a groaning and creaking noise, followed by the sharp sudden snap of wellies penetrating vulnerable thin ice. A splash, and another shocking splash. Rhys's terrified screams echoed all around the pond, but with the frosty surrounding area deserted, no one else could hear him. Only his brother.

Standing motionless on a nearby heather mound, Jason peered out from his parka hood. He kept his hands in his pockets as he observed his sibling's distress, fascinated, amused - and pleased. Always a spiteful child, not a muscle moved as Jason stared expressionless at his brother's desperate grasps. His useless woollen gloves made frantic clawing motions, polishing the hard shiny surface before he disappeared from view.

Rhys's wellies, parka hood and rubber-lined pockets filled with water. The rest of his clothes sponged up more pints, all combining to drag him under the freezing water. He emerged for a moment, gasping from the surprise and frigid shock, yet somehow his lungs helped produce a desperate scream for help. Rhys summoned up all the strength and energy his tiny body could muster. Instinctively kicking his legs, his wellies dropped away under the surface, giving him the impetus to place an elbow then a knee on the ice. He appeared to have rescued himself. But once again the ice snapped, and he lost his energy-sapping battle to gravity for a second and final time.

Three yards to the side of the vacant ice hole, a bare hand pressed upwards against the underside of the frozen barrier. Then a face. Then nothing. Jason Price never saw the face of his little brother again after that moment.

Within a year of the tragic *accidental* event, the Price family moved away from Blaenavon, without ever uncovering the truth about what happened to their youngest son. After Rhys's funeral, amidst speculation and local tongues wagging, moving away became the only option for them to put the past behind them.

~

Jason Price's next visit to the Keepers Pond came forty-nine years later. He passed by in his Range

Rover, his responsibility for the dreadful incident and his poor brother's screams for help barely registered, erased, as he stared impassively across the moors. He gave a cursory sideways glance towards the expanse of water, more interested in admiring the mountain ponies and scenic views stretching out towards Crickhowell and Brecon than recollecting Rhys's last gasps of life.

Price had more important things on his mind than a younger brother wiped from his memory five decades ago.

Chapter 2

The Olive's Evidence

Cardiff, Wales - November 2021

S orry Lauren, I don't understand, is there something wrong with the Zoom connection? Or could it be because I'm on Australian time and half asleep? Did you say they fired you for eating an olive? Darling, you work in a pizza parlour. How can they fire anyone for eating an olive for God's sake?"

"Mum, it's complicated. And it wasn't even a whole olive, just half of one. I could hardly keep my eyes open, and my stomach wouldn't stop rumbling. I did a shift at the bakery in town last night, got four hours sleep, went to Uni for one early rubbish lecture and then started a lunch shift at Luigi's. To make matters worse my one-to-one at Uni made me late, and Luigi's is in Cardiff Bay, so I needed a taxi to make it over there in time. Today's been crap. End of."

"I'm worried about you, you're overdoing it. You know we can wire you some more money if you need it, you only have to ask. How much do you need?"

"Mum I'm fine for money, honestly, well apart from the obvious. Look, everyone, my age has a Uni-fee overdraft, though not as big as mine. And *I* decided to do a *Masters* in the UK, nobody forced me to come here and do it. It seemed like a great idea at the time, and most of the time it is. I just hate 'Two-for-One-Wednesdays' that's all."

Lauren's mother remained concerned, "So how did you come to lose your job all of a sudden, what happened? I mean all over an olive. Sorry, half an olive?"

"Mum, you won't believe this. As usual, a typically chaotic day, non-stop with customers and kids when a young couple came in. They sat down and ordered a large pepperoni pizza to share. So, fifteen minutes later the service bell pinged, and as I picked up the pizza from *the pass* servery to take it to their table, I spotted an olive, *the olive*, with my name on it. I plucked it up and ate it, carried on walking, and plonked the pizza down on their table. As soon as I did, I spotted a long saggy string of mozzarella stretching from my chin to their pizza. I nearly died. They both looked at me. I looked at them. I wiped my chin and ran off."

Lauren could see the transformation in her mother's mortified face at the other end of the Zoom call. The screen appeared as though it had frozen with her mother's mouth stuck wide open. Moments later her shoulders shook uncontrollably as she made an unsuccessful attempt to contain fits of laughter with her head bowed and face in her hands.

She wiped tears from the corner of each eye, and said, "Well you always did love cheese, but when did you develop a taste for olives, I had no idea?"

"It's not funny Mum, but you're right I love cheese, although I seem to have gone off olives; can't understand why. So they decided to call the manager over and when I ended my shift, he finished me up. Nightmare."

"Oh Lauren, never mind love. Hey, Gran asked about you, I told her you are fine, but she's not remembering much. I tell her the same things every time I speak with her. I told her you're home for a few weeks next year for Olivia's wedding."

"Mum, next time you see her, go in the morning and we can all share a Zoom. Just let me know. But I'll see her soon anyway, can't wait to see you all, even if it is only for a couple of weeks. I'm so sorry I can't be there for Christmas - December flights are three times the price and I need the hours and the tips. I'll be home for Christmas next year I promise. Besides, the wedding will be more exciting than Christmas. A few months will fly by, I can't wait, I've missed all of you so much."

~

Over the next few days, Lauren Eaves settled back into her hard-working routine, studying, and enjoying

Wales. She also found a new waitressing job the next day in the bustling and vibrant city of Cardiff. She studied at Cardiff University for an MSc in Geology and Business Management and needed to crack on with her dissertation, and then she would have to start thinking about finding *that* amazing job.

Cardiff seemed like the perfect location to continue her studies. As an English speaking steppingstone to explore Europe, it also provided a highly regarded faculty and the career pathway course she needed. Lauren loved her grandparents, who originated from the Welsh valleys, and she promised them she would learn more about where they came from and grew up. A handful of distant cousins had already made contact with her on social media.

She possessed a drive and determination to help fund the AUS$40k per annum university fee, and the associated lifestyle debt racked up over the past few years studying in Sydney, and now Cardiff. Although young, bright, enthusiastic, and confident, the AUS$200k total debt never strayed far from Lauren's mind.

Her parents, Harry, and Margaret were not super-wealthy people – far from it. They owned a small arable farm and a three-man gold mining operation back in Western Australia, one of the reasons Lauren chose to study geology. Many years ago, the business thrived. They did all right, but the mining aspect had declined in recent times, and breaking even every year became a luxury. In many mines similar to theirs, the return-on-investment business models began to show smaller and smaller returns of gold per tonne of raw unprocessed material. The running costs to work longer shifts with more manpower just to keep heads above water kept increasing. The future for the family business over the next few years looked bleak. Lauren had an inkling of their difficulties. She worried about how tough things were becoming for her parents and wished she could do more to help them.

Chapter 3

Speculative Issues

Spain – Mid-December 2021

Jason Price had made a significant fortune as a land and commercial property speculator. Over the years he had experienced many ups and downs. From humble beginnings with a construction company in Cardiff, going bust twice in the early days, before landing on his feet with the success of small infrastructure and industrial developments.

These days he preferred to focus on high-quality office blocks and luxury retail complexes. He either retained them and acted as landlord through one of his various companies or sold them as assets to specialist pension fund investors. The formula performed well in the UK, and with the help of trusted international property management advisers, he embarked on similar projects with a recent expansion into Spain, whilst setting up a home there in 2019.

The uncharted waters of the Spanish commercial market meant Price needed to start cautiously, but he soon experienced great success thanks to a more relaxed regulatory regime. Things culminated in late October 2021, as he moved into his new home – two months before his sixtieth birthday party – when a major opportunity emerged, and Price seized it.

One of his property management agents tipped him off, "Jason, you asked me to give you a heads up if something special came up. Well, guess what – here it is. Something happened this morning and you need to jump on it."

Price's ears pricked up, "What is it?"

The agent gave Price the brief, "A large piece of premium location land, once earmarked as a golf complex on the edge of Barcelona. The golf land deal fell through, all because the investors concluded that more than enough golf courses existed in the region and got cold feet."

Price pressed for more information, "How big is large?"

The agent explained, "Local planners have decided to carve up one-hundred-and-fifty acres and develop it into smaller retail, commercial and residential projects. This is good timing for you to make a bid and grab a piece, Jason."

"Perfect." Price identified a thirty-acre plot as a development target and made his move.

A slight problem existed; with money tied up in other projects, he didn't have the liquid cash or credit line to raise all the necessary funds to buy the land and build what he wanted. But he knew a man who did, someone who often expressed an interest in diversifying into bigger ventures - if they came along - his new minor shareholder, Declan Ryan.

Price and Dubliner Ryan originally met through mutual social acquaintances, during the summer of 2020. Then in October 2021, Price bought his new house, from Ryan, and as part of the house deal secured a modest stake in Price's business. The 'stake' knocked a big hole in the price of the €3M house and Ryan gained himself the exposure he had been looking for to enter the commercial property speculation business.

They occasionally played golf together and were friendly, though often competed for vocal bandwidth in café and bar group conversations. Price's window of opportunity for the 'thirty-acre project' needed investment within weeks. A profit margin worth millions depended on it. Other potential investment candidates existed but Price narrowed it down to the most obvious man - Ryan.

For most businesspeople, Ryan's name wouldn't have appeared near the top of their lists. Price understood the concerns of others having picked up snippets from friends about Ryan's international haulage business. Some suggested for decades he and his family hauled anything too hot for others to handle. One or two suspected Ryan was a drugs cartel baron but said nothing.

Price thought jealous people love to sensationalise and embellish with fake news. So he took most of it with a pinch of salt, remaining undaunted. Ryan seemed a wealthy legitimate businessman and family man. With years of experience, a successful entrepreneur like Price expected all businesspeople to sail close to the wind from time to time, including himself - though sometimes preferring to plough straight through the wind at ramming speed. He enjoyed the financial returns and thrived on the adrenalin associated with the occasional risky decisions of running a business. Whilst Ryan's attention flattered Price, he possessed a low opinion of some of the other people he dealt with, in particular anyone who didn't agree with his ideas. Although stealing the ideas of other people and claiming them as his happened almost every week.

The thirty-acre project would yield spectacular returns; Ryan acknowledged Price's expertise and the idea of becoming a property magnate offered great appeal to him. Both agreed on the potential of a partnership, and the urgency required by the timing led to the pair having a long conversation. It resulted in Ryan agreeing to consider funding five times more than Price for the former golf course land, with more to follow for the construction work. This meant that Ryan would progress from being a minor shareholder in Price's Spanish business to a significant major shareholder.

"Jason, taking a small stake in some of your existing established business is one thing, a good thing.

This casino thing is on another level. My pockets are deep, but even I will be digging deep on this one to see it all the way through. I need to speak to my financial advisors and family first, I won't mess you around, so give me a couple of days."

Ryan didn't need to speak with anyone, he kept millions in some accessible clean and laundered savings and investments. The agreement in principle fell into place forty-eight hours later, with clauses built-in exposing Jason Price to big penalties if things didn't go according to plan. Ryan's bankrolling of Price also came with a menacing personal interpretation of what 'penalty' meant.

The Lucidity Programme
– JM Bayliss

The past has found its voice.

An incredible 74-year-old scientific mystery suddenly re-emerges. The British government is running out of ideas and time to solve a major threat to national security. Two elderly sisters in an Oxfordshire nursing home have 'put their affairs in order'. They pass a dangerous family secret to the government, a secret which could potentially leave the world defenceless to unstable or hostile governments. Wil is an unassuming farmer whose lucid dreams are being hijacked by voices from the past. He is inadvertently led into a series of exploits before coming to the attention of Government Communications HQ. He becomes their last hope in the search for the scientific discovery of the century. He naively steps up, not realising the full extent of the sacrifices he may have to make.

Available as paperback or e-book.

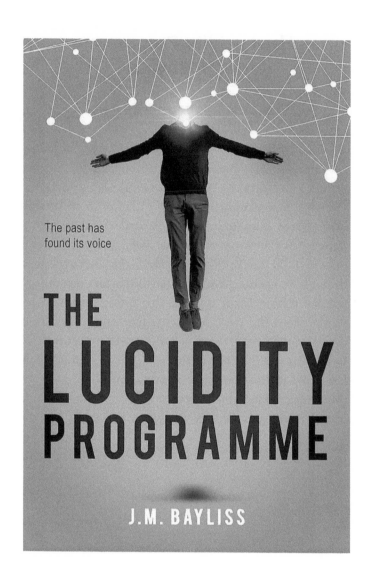

The past has
found its voice

THE
LUCIDITY
PROGRAMME

J.M. BAYLISS

The Lucidity Programme

Chapter 1 – Change the Dynamic

Review Meeting, Cheltenham – May 2019

"How long before *they* beat us to it, and find it, Phil? The PM will ask me later. What's your best guess?"

"Three months, less than a year if we're lucky. Unthinkable. *Unthinkable.* We'll get there – we must." Chalk replied.

"Christ." The Defence Secretary ended the call.

One hour earlier. Chalk had entered the second-floor meeting room. He was neither military nor ministerial, but commanded huge respect – they all stood.

Seated inside the room, which overlooked a manicured inner courtyard garden, were five women and three men. All, silent, other than for a distracting fizz caused by the filling of some glasses with Buxton's finest. Blank faces, deep in thought, as they struggled to present positive facades. Some made last-minute checks on laptops and tablets of inadequate facts or figures that didn't add up. An emotive meeting agenda confronted them – a serious threat to British national security, and global peace.

On the south-west edge of Cheltenham sits an eye-catching, ring-shaped building. At six-hundred feet in diameter, seventy feet high, set on one-hundred-and-seventy-six acres, surrounded by dedicated car parks and the highest security imaginable. This modern, spectacular piece of architecture is GCHQ – the UK government's General Communications Headquarters, or 'Eavesdropping Central' to the locals.

The building's affectionate nickname is 'The Doughnut'. Often working in collaboration with the military, security services, police forces and friendly foreign governments, GCHQ keeps the UK safe from all kinds of problems within our own country and abroad.

Employed inside are an eclectic mix of over four thousand well-organised, highly-focused academics – linguists, mathematicians, cryptologists, analysts, and researchers. GCHQ also advertises to recruit hackers and mavericks, to address the growth industry of cybercrime.

GCHQ hosted some regular visitors from DSTL – Defence Science and Technology Laboratory – the government's famous scientific department based in Porton Down near Salisbury.

Together, they strived for answers for weeks after someone had passed DSTL some astonishing, technological information that needed GCHQ assistance to validate its authenticity and help solve a puzzle. Something, if genuine, would be a serious and dangerous threat to NATO forces and defence systems.

The team of senior people had reached an impasse and were getting nowhere. They suspected other interested parties around the world had become aware of the information and might be trying to solve the same conundrum. The obvious concern focused on their competitor's progress. Did *they* have better intelligence than DSTL?

Chalk, of DSTL, concluded, "Guys, we will find the answers – as always. We have excellent resources, support from Westminster, and the best people - all working together. We don't stop. We keep going. We continue searching for something or someone to help us – we do not give up."

He remained confident, defiant, that they would find the answers and a solution – at some point – but when. The risk associated with losing the race to a hostile or unstable foreign government was unthinkable.

Their pool of ideas needed refreshing and topping up. So far, all of their usual impeccable standards and successful investigation methods had failed to resolve the situation confronting them. They needed a fresh approach, something special to happen to change the dynamic.

# # #

Dear Reader, if you enjoyed chapter one of The Lucidity Programme, you may be interested to know that the short story called 'A Glimmer', which you may have read earlier, also happens to be Chapters Two and Three of The Lucidity Programme. This introduces the main characters Wil and Emma. I hope you will read and enjoy the rest of the book. Thank you – Mark Bayliss

Lightning Source UK Ltd.
Milton Keynes UK
UKHW010803230622
404852UK00008B/404